CAN'T
TRANSITIONS
TO CAN
WITH A FRIEND WHO'S TRUE BLUE

Written by Leah Irby

Illustrated by Jessica Gamboa

 FriesenPress

One Printers Way
Altona, MB R0G 0B0
Canada

www.friesenpress.com

ISBN
978-1-03-911069-4 (Hardcover)
978-1-03-911068-7 (Paperback)
978-1-03-911070-0 (eBook)

1. *Juvenile Fiction, LGBT*

Distributed to the trade by The Ingram Book Company

For E. I.

May you always feel free
to jump so high
you touch the sky.

For E. I. B.

Thanks for creating
the rainbow road

and inspiring
everyone with your joy.

Part 1.

One day a turtle the color of blue
was sitting around with nothing to do.
She saw a red ant, a possible friend,
as the ant came walking around the bend.

"Hello, I'm the turtle who's named **True Blue.**
What is your name?
I'm so glad to meet you."

The ant stopped to think about what to reveal.

Should I say my birth name or the one that I feel?

When I look at myself, I see so much red,

but I wish I was indigo-colored instead.

I don't know if this turtle is really true blue.

"My name is **Can't.**

It's nice to meet you."

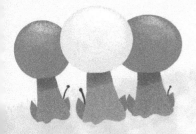

"Come," said the turtle who was

True Blue.

"Let's find together, something to do.

How 'bout we try to jump so high,

so high, so high _we touch the sky?"_

Can't the red ant wasn't sure what to say.

Even red ants can't jump in that way.

"Ants aren't meant to jump so high,

so high, so high _we touch the sky."_

"What do you mean?"
asked **True Blue.**

"Do you need me to give lessons to you?

How do you know that *you can't touch the sky?*

How do you know if you don't dare to try?"

"I learned how to jump from my wise and dear friend
Glad Gold the grasshopper, **Glad** to the end.

Grasshoppers love to jump way up high,"
True Blue the turtle now said with a sigh.

"The grasshopper was a **Glad Gold** gem

and said I should try, just like them.

Glad told me they could jump so high,

so high, so high **they touched the sky.**"

"At the start, I was worried what I would
feel. What if I hurt myself, for real?
I didn't think turtles could jump so high,
so high, so high **we touch the sky.**"

"**Glad** didn't give up or go right away.
They kept asking to come, jump and play!
But I was still worried what others would think,
so I said, '**GO AWAY!**' with bold bright ink."

"**Glad Gold** the grasshopper
jumped up and down,
patiently waiting without any frown,
waiting for me to jump so high,
so high, so high *I touch the sky.*"

"**Glad** waited and waited, did not go away.
They listened to me as I sat all the day.
I decided that they were a **true friend,**
someone on whom I could surely depend."

"**Glad Gold** the grasshopper
jumped up so high,
so high I thought *they touched the sky.*
I asked what it feels like to jump about.
I asked what it feels like not to have doubt."

"**Glad Gold** the grasshopper smiled and said,
'You must see yourself jumping first in your head.
You won't know what it's like without trying it out.
You won't know what it's like without losing your doubt.'"

"Then one morning,
my day to jump came.

Ready to leap, I finally took aim.

When I did jump,
I tripped and I fell.
My foot got so hurt
that it started to **swell**."

"Slithering out of the forest there came
Sparkle the snake to help with my pain.
This healer that all of the animals knew
sang a soft song so my foot would feel new."

"Now I ran, and I jumped, and for once it was true.

I sprang off the ground; it was long overdue.

I thought to myself when I didn't fall,

'Wow, that was fun!'

I was having a ball!"

"I did it! I jumped! It felt great to be

there with my friend, gladly cheering for me.

Glad taught me to jump and how to believe

that if I keep trying, one day I'll succeed."

"That was the moment, the moment I knew

that if I keep trying, my dream will come true.

There will be a day I can jump so high,

so high, so high

I touch the sky!"

"**Can't** are you ready to **jump and feel free?**

Come let's practice,

just you and me."

Can't thought—I'm scared. How should I tell

that my name does not match who I am very well?

"Can't" I don't like—or the pronoun of **"he."**

How do I say that I really am **"she?"**

Unless I can figure a different way through,

I'm called **Red** (like stop), so that's what I'll do.

"Is there anything else at all I can do,
to make you feel comfortable?" asked **True Blue.**
"I promise to be with you all of the way,
so we can together jump the whole day!"
Can't the red ant had to pause for a bit
and chose to continue to think about it.
"For today, I will say that you are a **true friend,**
someone on whom
I can surely depend."

Part 2.

"Today's a new day," said the turtle, **True Blue.**

"We can jump any hurdle, together us two.

Let's see if we can jump so high,

so high, so high *we touch the sky!*"

"I can't," said **Can't** the red ant with a frown.

"I don't want to somehow end up upside down.

Ants aren't meant to jump and play.

Ants are meant to carry all day."

"The only thing **Can't,** that is truer than true, whatever you think that you can't or can do, either one's right as you think on a theme,

So make sure your words always fit with your dream.

Now close your ant eyes and see from inside.

Can you see yourself jump, saying you tried?"

"As much as I try, with all of my might, the picture's unclear. It doesn't seem right."

"I feel on the inside, the feeling of sad.

I can't try new things with the name that I have.

But, I won't know what it's like without trying it out.

I won't know what it's like without losing my doubt."

With big tears in her eyes, **Can't** looked at her friend.

"Are you truly someone on whom I can depend?"
True Blue reached out to hug **Can't** on that day.

"No matter what, I'm your friend here to stay."

"'**Can't** the red ant' can't describe who I am.
I now shall be called the ant, **Indigo Can**.
They called me by 'he,' but I truly am 'she,'
and this color of red
I will shed as I'm free."

True Blue now said without reservation, "No matter the thoughts of the rest of our nation, I believe and support you, all the way through.

I, **True Blue** the turtle, will always **love you.**" "You **can** jump so high that you touch the sky. You **can** do the things that you dream to try. We **can** call you 'She!' Oh yes we can! We **can** call you 'Her!' Oh yes we can!"

Glad Gold told us, "When we're on the brink,
we must ask the right questions and stop to think.
No more of saying, 'I can't jump. Why?'

'How,' we must ask,
'should I now touch the sky?'"

Can pictured it clearly, right there in her mind.
"I can see myself touching the sky, in due time.
I **know** that I can. I must try my own way.

I can see my light shining
as bright as the day."

Indigo Can opened up her big eyes.
"Thank you, **True Blue**, what a pleasant surprise
to have a friend happily cheering for me,
when others can't see me as I'm meant to be."
Can got so excited, she let her voice out.
She got so excited, she started to shout.

"I'm she, her, herself!
That's who I am!
I'm she, her, herself.
No more feeling less-than!"

Blaze
the butterfly
then fluttered in,
and **Clear Dreamer** the dragonfly came with a spin.
Brawn the red beetle and **Glad Gold** came running.
They saw this ant, **Can**, who was looking quite stunning.

As **Sparkle** the snake
came slithering by,
Can couldn't help it, she started to cry.

"You are all so supportive of me being me.
I'm so happy, so happy at last to feel free."
Sparkle at once started softly to chant
as the others joined in to encourage the ant.

"Let's practice your pronouns, together we can.

'She, her, herself!' Oh yes, we sure can!"

Can spun around,
as the light shone through.
Can spun around,
'til the light was true.

Without looking 'round,
centered feet on the ground,
Can took a deep breath,

jumping up and back down.

True Blue was oh so excited to see **Can** so happy, as happy Can be.

"You are shining your light and you jumped way up high. You showed off your might and **you can touch the sky.**"

As **Can** tried to talk
to those who saw her jump,
her words stuck in her throat,
like a gigantic lump.
But the animals all waited for her to speak.
They supported her change, not making a tweak.
"Let's help each other to listen and see—
your image is vital to who you must be.

So let your light shine
from inside to out,

and never give up
even if you
have doubt."

Dear reader,

My name is **Leah**, and my pronouns are **she/her**. Please know that you are unique and important, even if your gender or pronouns are not represented by one of the characters in this series. We need all the genders to make our rainbow shine. Just like the characters in the story, people use different pronouns to help others understand who they are. Some examples are: he, she, they, and ze. They and ze are pronouns used for a singular person whose gender identity doesn't fit the label of only male or only female.

Some people have a gender that does not change. Some are gender-fluid which means they identify with different genders on different days or at different times in their lives. Some people take time to understand and explain their gender to others. So, don't get upset if a friend explains their gender differently from what you thought before.

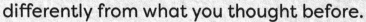

There is no right or wrong way to understand your own gender, but we do need to respect others by using the pronouns that they ask us to. When someone calls you by a name that is not correct, it can make you feel upset. People also get upset when you use incorrect pronouns for them. If you don't know someone's pronouns, you can use "they/them" pronouns to refer to them until you know. Do you have a set of pronouns that you feel best matches your identity?

Try this out:

"My name is _____.
And my pronouns are _____."

Would you like to hear some music to go with the story and discover more educational materials? Scan this QR code with your smartphone, or go to https://www.leahirby.com/gender-rainbow.

About the Author

 Leah Irby remarked to her future husband, when first meeting him on the dance floor, that she could see herself living in Stockholm someday. With a detour first to India, her life would eventually take her to Sweden where she lives with her family today. Leah spent many years as an orchestra teacher in the United States, helping children find their unique voice and a place to belong. Dancing lindy hop, playing viola, and hanging out with swans are a few of her favorite things. As a solo recording artist, she continues to use music to heal and inspire.

About the Illustrator

Jessica Gamboa creates art from her home in Argentina, but dreams of traveling the world with her pencil, watercolors and digital canvas. She graduated from art school in Buenos Aires with a focus on children's book illustration. She is the illustrator of *Noodle Monster* by Sarah Quirk and half a dozen other stories.

CPSIA information can be obtained
at www.ICGtesting.com
Printed in the USA
BVHW022146161221
624079BV00004B/62